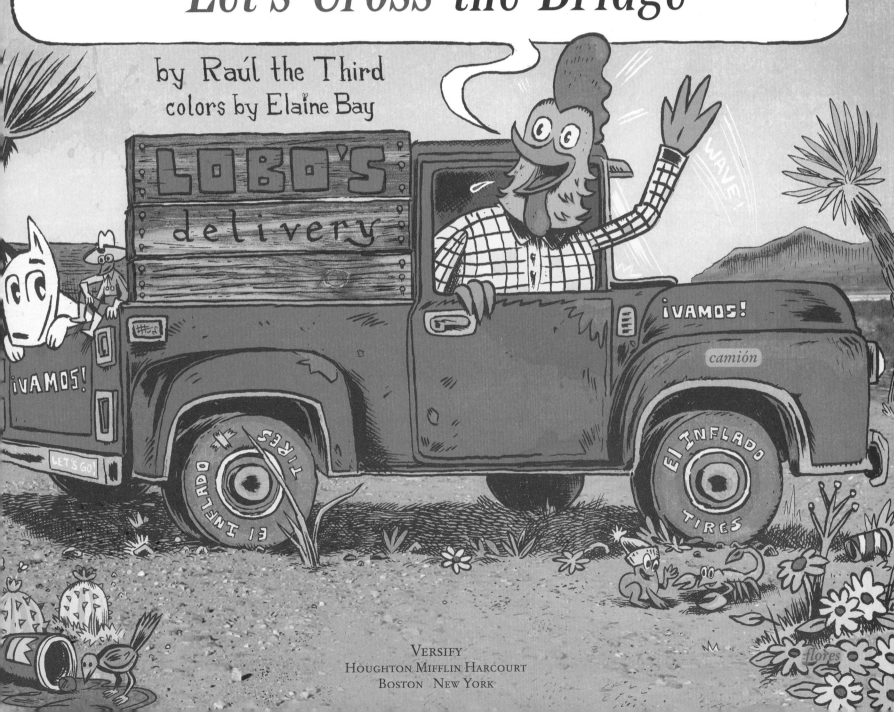

¡VAMOS!

Let's Cross the Bridge

by Raúl the Third
colors by Elaine Bay

VERSIFY
HOUGHTON MIFFLIN HARCOURT
BOSTON NEW YORK

To my family's old blue Astro van that was always overheating.
You were a nightmare, but I'll never forget you.
—Raúl

To all of the people who build bridges
and to the brave people who cross them
—Elaine

Versify® is an imprint of Houghton Mifflin Harcourt Publishing Company.
Versify is a registered trademark of Houghton Mifflin Harcourt Publishing Company.

hmhbooks.com

The illustrations in this book were done in ink on smooth plate
Bristol board with Adobe Photoshop for color.
The text type was set in Stempel Garamond LT Std.
The display type was set in Latin MT Std.
Hand lettering by Raúl Gonzalez

The Library of Congress Cataloging-in-Publication Data is on file.
ISBN: 978-0-358-38040-5

Manufactured in China
SCP 10 9 8 7 6 5 4 3 2 1
4500824313

La Celebración is across the river in a city in another country.

¡Veo el puente!
I see the bridge!

At night, from high above, the two cities on either side of the bridge look like one big city.

Every day, thousands of people cross from one side of the bridge to the other. They go to work, shop, and visit family and friends.

They cross by car,

by truck,

monumento

on foot,

and by skateboard.

On one side of the bridge most people speak Spanish and on the other most speak English, but . . . lots of people in both places speak both languages!

Many people are working on the bridge.

Mal Burro and Peeky Pequeño are washing people's windshields.

Some are selling snacks to hungry drivers.

Everywhere they look, there is something new to see.

So many vehicles putter in place,

waiting for their turn to cross the bridge.

As the day turns to night . . .

Hearing Kooky's call, all the food trucks on the bridge turn on their ovens.

Everyone begins to dance.
Los bailarines folklóricos show off their dance moves.

The lowriders hip and hop.

Señor Puppetro puts on a show.

And last but not least . . .

El Toro and his friends help Little Lobo hang up all the piñatas!

With candy raining down on the crowds,
Little Lobo sets off his fireworks.

That night, on a bridge between two countries, La Celebración came to everyone.

GLOSSARY*

*These are only some of the words found in Little Lobo's story. Be sure to look up other ones you don't know in a Spanish-English dictionary!

(El) Águila – Eagle
(El) Autobús – Bus
(El) Avión – Plane
(El) Baile – Dance
(La) Bota – Boot
(El) Camión – Truck
(La) Camioneta – Van
(La) Canción – Song
(El) Cascabel – Rattle
(El) Cemento – Cement
(Las) Chispas – Sparkles
(El) Chivo – Goat
(El) Cinto – Belt
(El) Claxon – Horn
(El) Coche – Car
(El) Cofre – Car hood
(El) Dulce – Candy
(Las) Estrellas – Stars
(El) Faro – Headlight
(Las) Flores – Flowers
(El) Fuego – Fire

(El) Gallo – Rooster
(El) Hueso – Bone
(La) Luna – Moon
(La) Luz – Light
(El) Maullido – Meow
(El) Monumento – Monument
(La) Mosca – Fly
(La) Motocicleta – Motorcycle
Ocho – Eight
(El) Paracaídas – Parachute
(La) Patineta – Skateboard
(La) Ranita – Little frog
Rápido – Fast
(El) Río – River
(El) Sol – Sun
(El) Telescopio – Telescope
(La) Trompeta – Trumpet
(El) Viaje – Trip
(La) Viejita – Little old lady
(Los) Zancos – Stilts

paracaídas

A NOTE FROM RAÚL THE THIRD

MI MAMÁ was born in Mexico City in 1954, and when she turned thirteen, she and her family moved to Ciudad Juárez. With her family, she worked at the Mercado Cuauhtémoc, selling a wide array of crafts and goods. Juárez is a Mexican border town, and across the river in the United States is a city named El Paso in Texas. My dad grew up in a community in El Paso called Ysleta, which was settled in 1680. When he was twenty-one, he visited the Mercado Cuauhtémoc and immediately fell in love with mi mamá. A few short months later they were married.

I was the first of three boys born in El Paso, Texas, and for me El Paso and Juárez were one giant city filled with family and friends. I remember waiting at the bus stop with my mom and brothers as we began our journey to Juárez to visit family at the mercado. Once we arrived in downtown El Paso, we would go through the turnstile and begin crossing the bridge into Juárez.

The bridge was built over the Río Grande, and sometimes we crossed it by foot and other times we went in the car. The bridge was a magical place, with people walking or driving back and forth. If you drove over the bridge, you were greeted by street vendors, windshield washers, performers, and all sorts of interesting people and cars.

We crossed the bridge to visit family and loved ones, to work, to play, and to shop. The bridge connected us to our dreams and to the possibilities they contained. The bridge was our link to our past and to the future it has helped create, and each time I crossed it, I celebrated the long journey of my ancestors.